John Brown, Rose and the Midnight Cat

Story by Jenny Wagner

Illustrations by Ron Brooks

Bradbury Press
Scarsdale, New York

Special thanks to Bob Sessions
R.B.

Text Copyright © 1977 by Jenny Wagner
Illustrations Copyright © 1977 by Ron Brooks

ISBN: 0-87888-120-4

Rose's husband died a long time ago.
Now she lived with her dog.
His name was John Brown.

John Brown loved Rose,
and he looked after her in every way he could.

In summer he sat under the pear tree with her.

In winter he watched as she dozed by the fire.
All year round he kept her company.

'We are all right, John Brown,' said Rose.
'Just the two of us, you and me.'

One night Rose looked out of the window
and saw something move in the garden.

'What's that in the garden, John Brown?' she said.
John Brown would not look.

'Out there,' said Rose. 'I think it's a cat.'
'I don't see any cat,' said John Brown.

'I'm sure it's a cat. Go and give it some milk.'
'There's nobody there,' said John Brown.

But that night, when Rose was safe in bed,
John Brown went outside.
He drew a line around the house

Then Rose got up and sat by the fire, for a while.
And the midnight cat sat on the arm of the chair…

and purred.

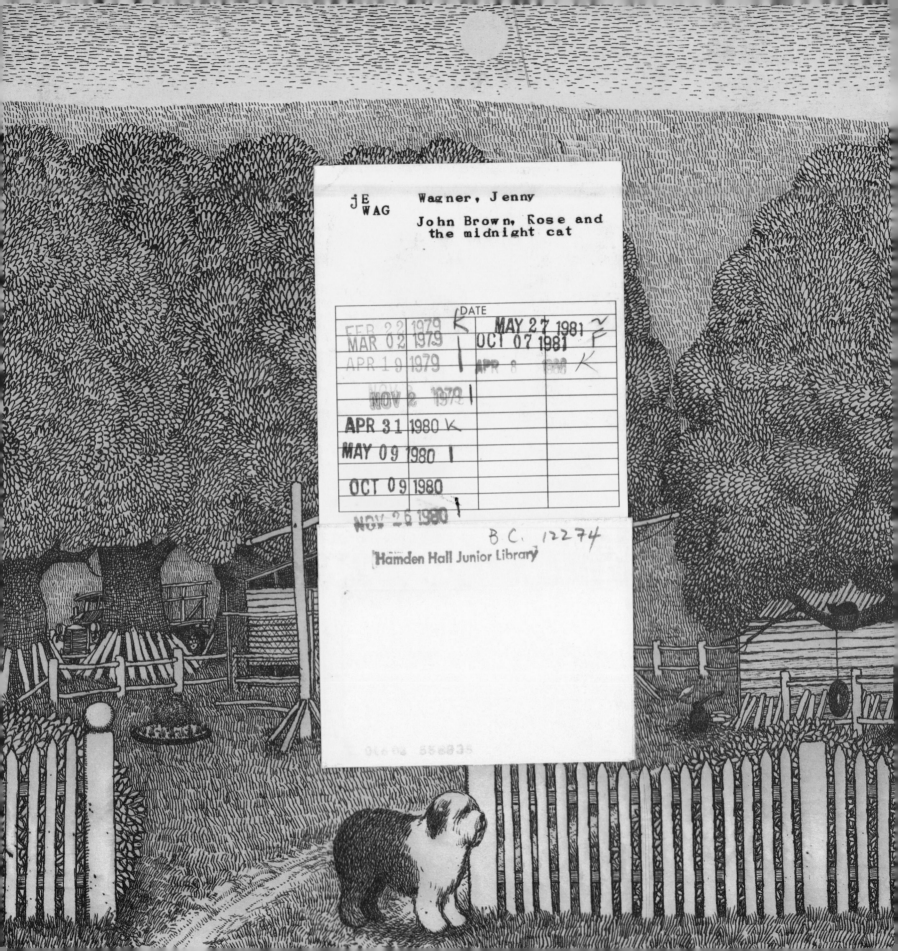

and told the midnight cat to stay away.
'We don't need you, cat,' he said.
'We are all right, Rose and I.'

The next night Rose saw the midnight cat
as he slipped through the shadow of the pear tree.
'Look, there he is, John Brown,' she said.
'Don't you see him now?'
But John Brown shut his eyes.

Rose sighed and packed up her knitting.
Then she wound up the clock and took the milk bottles out.
John Brown followed her.
'I'm sure there's no cat.' he said.

And every night, when Rose was not looking,
John Brown tipped it out again.

'You don't need a cat,' he said.

'You've got me.'

One night the midnight cat jumped up at the window
and rubbed his back against the glass.
His eyes were like lamps,
and his fur shone against the ragged sky.

'Look, John Brown!' said Rose. 'Isn't he beautiful?
Get up and let him in.'
'No!' said John Brown, and pulled the curtains shut.
'No, I won't let him in.'

Next morning Rose did not get up.
John Brown waited in the kitchen for his breakfast,
and nothing happened.

He went to see what was wrong.
'I'm sick,' said Rose. 'I'm staying in bed.'
'All day?' said John Brown.
'All day and for ever,' said Rose.

John Brown thought.
He thought all through lunch time

and when supper time came, he was still thinking.

An hour past supper time he went back to Rose,
and woke her gently.

'Will the midnight cat make you better?' he asked.
'Oh yes!' said Rose. 'That's just what I want.'

John Brown went out to the kitchen and opened the door,
and the midnight cat came in.